Meet The Little Charmers

by Jenne Simon

© Spin Master Charming Productions Inc., 2014,
All rights reserved. ® and © Nelvana Limited.
™Corus Entertainment Inc.
All rights reserved. Used under license by Scholastic Inc.

Scholastic Children's Books,
Euston House, 24 Eversholt Street,
London NW1 1DB, UK

A division of Scholastic Ltd
London ~ New York ~ Toronto ~ Sydney ~ Auckland
Mexico City ~ New Delhi ~ Hong Kong

First published in the US by Scholastic Inc, 2015
SCHOLASTIC and associated logos are trademarks and/or registered trademarks of Scholastic Inc.
Published in the UK by Scholastic Ltd, 2016

ISBN 978 1407 16408 3

Printed in Malaysia

2 4 6 8 10 9 7 5 3 1

Papers used by Scholastic Children's Books are made from woods grown in sustainabl

Book design by Erin McMahon

www.scholastic.co.uk

1

Welcome to Charmville,

where every day is full of magic! Hazel, Posie and Lavender are three best friends who can't wait to learn how to use their brand-new magical abilities. The Little Charmers love helping their friends and family. But sometimes their magic ends up creating problems instead of solving them. Using the magic of teamwork and friendship, Hazel, Posie and Lavender always manage to fix things again.

Turn the page to meet the Charmers - in - Training and explore their world of enchantment!

Meet Hazel

Little Charmer Hazel has a big heart and loves her best friends to bits! She is thrilled to learn magic and adores trying out new spells. It's a good thing she has her very own – and very powerful – glittery magic wand.

With just a few special words, Hazel's wand can do almost anything. But it takes more than a wand to make magic happen. Hazel uses her own special magic to add the finishing touches to all the Charmers' spells.

Swizzle and fizzle,
do your SPARKLING best.
Duster and broom,
CLEAN UP
this mess!

5

Hazel has good intentions and a big heart. She makes mistakes sometimes but she always cleans up her messes.

Magical Speciality:

Animal Whisperer. She has an amazing ability to understand and translate what an animal is saying.

Pet:

Seven the Cat

Favourite Accessory:

Her glittery and magical star wand!

Likes:

Her friends, her family, magic and trying new things. Hazel adores a new challenge!

Dislikes:

Not having enough to do, letting people down, routine

Clickety-clackety twinkly joy.
Let flowers
BLOOM BRIGHT
for my friends
TO ENJOY!

8

Meet Posie™

Posie is a Spellerina. That means she's good at casting magic spells through her songs, which are always pitch-perfect. This Little Charmer thinks magic is much more fun when she's dancing to her own special beat. She carries an enchanted flute that can play every tune under the sun.

Posie loves nature more than anything else.
When she plays her flute, the flowers start to dance.
She can hear the wind sigh and the rain laugh. And she's
just as good at picking up on her friends' feelings.

Magical Speciality:

Spellerina – Posie has a spell and a song for every occasion!

Pet:

Treble the Owl

Favourite Accessory:

Her special magic flute wand

Likes:

Music, gardening, sunny days, rainy days and talking ... a lot!

Dislikes:

Not being with her friends, being stuck indoors, and not being able to help people

Meet Lavender

If Lavender mixes the right ingredients together, she can make magic! She's a Potionista, and her practical thinking helps her create amazingly cool potions and fabulously co-ordinated outfits. Lavender is logical and patient – two very important skills for any scientist and fashionista. She can follow potion recipes precisely and hunt down the perfect charm bracelet to match her latest fashion design.

A sparkly potion's the PERFECT MIX to make this outfit a MAGICAL FIX!

13

Just because Lavender is always perfectly put together doesn't mean she's afraid to get down and dirty. She'll wade through mud and muck, leaves and lizards to find the right ingredient for a potion.

Magical Speciality:

Potionista. Lavender is great at mixing potions – and patterns!

Pet:

Flare the Baby Dragon

Favourite Accessory:

A bubbly potion bottle wand that summons magic

Likes:

Following the rules, recipes, science and creating new fashion trends

Dislikes:

Uncertainty, not having a plan

Meet the Magical Pets

No Little Charmer's life would be complete without a *purr*-fect pet to share in her adventures! Hazel can talk to any animal, and her best friends, Posie and Lavender, don't need words to understand their furry friends, either.

TYPE OF ANIMAL: Cat
PERSONALITY: Independent, unpredictable, and mischievious. Seven has a mind of his own!

LITTLE CHARMER: Hazel
TALENT: Seven can always tell when Hazel's making a magical mistake.

Flare™

TYPE OF ANIMAL: Baby Dragon

PERSONALITY: Joker. Flare is a flying funster!

LITTLE CHARMER: Lavender

TALENT: Flare loves to laugh, but she's still learning to control her fire-breathing!

Treble™

TYPE OF ANIMAL: Owl

PERSONALITY: Wise and calm. She likes to watch the action from afar.

LITTLE CHARMER: Posie

TALENT: Treble sees danger coming from miles away, and zooms in when Posie needs her.

Explore the Charmhouse!

The Charmhouse is cosy, bright and cheerful – the perfect place for the Charmers-in-Training to hang out and practise their magic. It sits high up in a treetop without stairs or a rope ladder. So the Charmers must sing the Charmhouse entrance spell and skip up the magic hopscotch path to enter.

Inside the Charmhouse, the Little Charmers meet to mix potions, hold tea parties, have sleepovers and, most of all, have fun!

Hazel's

room has a cosy couch and lots of nooks and crannies for the girls and their pets to hang out in.

Lavender's

room is a Potionista's delight! She's got space to mix potions and design her latest fashions.

Posie's

room is like an indoor playground, complete with its own swing!

Meet Hazel's Parents

Mum

Hazel's sweet and hardworking mum is the Royal Empress of Charmville. She is devoted to her daughter and to helping the magical citizens of her town.

Dad

Hazel's dad is a Wizard who's both fun and funny. He spends his days fixing, designing and test-flying new brooms for his broom shop.

Meet Parsley

Posie's older brother, Parsley, is a Wizard-in-Training. He enjoys teasing the Charmers-in-Training – he has had a lot more magical practice than the Little Charmers. Parsley loves competing in Charmville's broom races – he's speedy and knows his way around a broomstick.

Meet Ferg, the Frog Prince

The Little Charmers un-frogged this adorable prince. He prefers being a frog to being a boy, but he adores Hazel, Lavender and Posie and is always willing to change back into a prince to help them out.

Every day in Charmville is a magical adventure! The Little Charmers try their hardest to improve their magical skills . . . and have sparktastic fun doing it. Their spells don't always go as planned. But as Hazel says, "It's not *where* the broom takes you, it's how you get there!"

LITTLE CHARMERS CHEER!

We wave our wands.
We play our wands.
We pour our special potions.
We sparkle up,
and cast a spell,
in a single charming motion!

SPARKLE UP, LITTLE CHARMERS!